Leland

© 2025 Shane Blakeslee

Cover and interior design by the author.
Printed in the United States of America.
First Edition

Contact: info@Lelandthebook.com

ISBN: *979-8-9990309-0-0*

V1.4

Leland

Remember. Always.

The Story

Leland Blakeslee was nineteen when his life ended—and everything else began.

He died in the Korean War—his future buried beneath a cold ridge near Unsan. But what if he had lived?

Leland is a stunning reimagining of the life that could have been. From a small town in Western New York to the forefront of innovation, this novel traces the arc of a brilliant mind who survives war, heals, loves, and quietly changes the world. He helps shape technologies that change how we live, brings light to homes across the globe, and asks the questions that would quietly reshape the future: What if every home made its own power? What if every veteran came home to open arms? What if retirement and healthcare were a birthright, not a privilege?

Told with lyrical depth, historical precision, and deep compassion, Leland is more than historical fiction—it's a meditation on loss, legacy, and the futures that live on in our imaginations.

It would have been a wonderful life.

CONTENTS

CONTENTS

CHAPTER 1

A SMALL TOWN BOY

IN THE SLEEPY oil-boom town of Bolivar, New York—population 2,600—life moved to the hum of oil pumps and the ringing of church bells. Nestled in the quiet, wooded hills of Allegany County near the Pennsylvania border, Bolivar was a town where the days were measured not by headlines or stock prices, but by weather patterns, local gossip, and the scent of supper drifting from open kitchen windows.

At 65 Plum Street, in a modest white clapboard house with green shutters and a porch that creaked like a familiar tune, Leland Frederick Blakeslee was born on June 28, 1931. A large sugar maple shaded the yard, blazing yellow and crimson each autumn and casting dappled shadows across the front steps in summer. The house smelled faintly of old wood, fresh-baked bread, and the linseed oil Merle used to clean his tools. This was the world into which Leland came screaming, squinting, and already curious.

The Blakeslees were a respected family. Merle, a maintenance supervisor at the Sinclair Oil refinery, was steady and soft-spoken, his hands permanently smudged with grease and grit. Belle, warm and sharp-witted, balanced motherhood with part-time work as an Avon lady, her voice a familiar knock at a dozen neighborhood doors. They raised four children with firm kindness, frugality, and deep belief in hard work: Barbara, the eldest, a natural caretaker with a gift for calming storms; Mac, who would join the Navy and chase adventure far from home; Leland, ever observant and precise; and Ronnie, the youngest, a spirited boy born in 1933 who idolized his older brother and followed him everywhere.

From the time he could walk, Leland dismantled the world to understand it. He took apart clocks, radios, and toasters—not always with the success of reassembly, much to Belle's chagrin, but always with dogged fascination. In Merle's garage workshop, he and Ronnie became pint-sized inventors. They repaired bicycles for neighbors, coaxed old lawnmowers back to life, and built contraptions from spare parts that occasionally whirred to life—or exploded with a puff of smoke and a lesson learned. Their golden retriever, Lady, lay beside them, one eye open, as the boys argued over screw sizes and soldering technique.

It was here, in the glow of a single bulb above Merle's workbench, that Leland's imagination first took root—not just in the machines, but in the belief that problems could be solved, and that even small tools in steady hands could build something great.

Leland was also a boy of faith and music. Every Sunday at 10:30 sharp, he attended the Bolivar Methodist Church, where he lit altar candles or rang the heavy bronze bell that echoed across the valley like a call to memory. He played alto saxophone in the Bolivar Central School band, rising to first chair by sophomore year, and sang tenor in the chorus with a clarity that startled many adults. He was more comfortable in the wings than the spotlight, but when he played, he played with soul.

In 1946, at fifteen, Leland was named scribe of Boy Scout Troop 39. His notebooks were meticulous, with carefully drawn maps, tidy attendance rosters, and records of every service project. His Scoutmaster praised him as steady and resourceful. His troop—Reginald Goodnoe, Jesse June, Ronnie Cline, Gordon George, and Neil

Dempsey—were his companions in adventure. Together they sledded down Water Tank Hill in winter until their cheeks were numb and their laughter breathless. Summers were for tree forts in the woods behind the school, for fishing along the Genesee, and for banana splits shared at the Sugar Bowl diner, a red-boothed haven with a jukebox and neon clock.

Leland was a fixture in town: shoveling snow from neighbors' steps before they could ask, mowing lawns for the elderly, helping set up folding chairs at the community center. His teachers described him as modest, fiercely intelligent, and unfailingly kind. He never boasted, but he carried an air of purpose that others noticed. During his junior year, he served as stage manager for the school play and built a pulley system that simulated a thunderstorm—complete with lightning flash and thunderclap. The audience gasped. Leland, backstage, simply adjusted the ropes.

And then there was Helen.

She was from Richburg, a town just a few miles down the road, and they met at a school dance arranged by mutual friends. She played piano, loved the night sky, and had a laugh that made Leland forget his shyness. They spent weekends walking the gorge trails of Letchworth State Park, talking about books, music, and dreams that reached far beyond Allegany County. Their romance was gentle and genuine—a hand held beneath the stars, a letter passed in church, a promise shared in the quiet hours of a late-summer drive.

In June of 1949, Leland took Helen to senior prom. He wore a borrowed tuxedo and drove the family Chevy Fleetmaster sedan. They danced to Glenn Miller, and when the band played "Moonlight Serenade," they stood on the gymnasium steps, looking out at the warm night. Under a canopy of stars, they made a promise—not of forever, not yet, but of keeping in touch, no matter what.

That same month, Leland graduated from Bolivar Central with high honors and a certificate of merit in science. His teachers urged him toward college. His parents hoped he would go. He had been accepted. But halfway across the world, conflict brewed.

On June 25, 1950, North Korean forces crossed the 38th parallel. But Leland had already made his choice.

CHAPTER 2

A CALL TO SERVE

On the morning of July 2, 1949, just weeks after his graduation, Leland Blakeslee stood on the steps of the Allegany County Courthouse and raised his right hand. The sun was already high, burning off the fog that clung to the hills, and the air carried the scent of summer grass and hot pavement. At eighteen, with his jaw set and eyes steady, he took the oath of enlistment.

"I do solemnly swear…"

He'd told no one but Helen of his decision, not even his parents, until the paperwork was signed. He wanted no fanfare. No persuasion. Just duty.

When he finally told them over dinner—Belle still in her apron, Merle wiping his hands on a Sinclair rag—there was a silence that seemed to stretch the length of the table. Belle's fork paused halfway to her mouth. Merle set down his glass with a slow, deliberate motion. Leland waited.

"I thought you were going to Cornell," his mother said quietly.

"I can still go. After." His voice was calm, but resolute. "I want to serve first."

Merle nodded once, slowly. Belle said nothing. But that night,

Leland heard muffled sobs behind the closed bedroom door. He didn't sleep. Neither did she.

By the end of July, he was on a train bound for Fort Dix, New Jersey. The fields of Western New York gave way to cities, then to barracks. The air smelled of metal and sweat. The days began before sunrise with the bark of drill sergeants and the sting of morning frost on concrete. Recruits were molded like clay—shaved, shouted at, broken down, built up. Leland's hands, once used for fine repairs and delicate wires, now learned the mechanics of rifles and the rhythm of forced marches. The Browning Automatic Rifle, or BAR, weighed almost 40 pounds loaded. Leland, barely 110 pounds himself, carried it without complaint.

"Why you?" someone asked him.

"Somebody has to," he replied. "Might as well be me."

He wrote home every Sunday. His letters were neat, sometimes humorous, but Helen noticed the distance between the lines. Belle saved everyone in a shoe box beneath her bed.

After fourteen weeks of basic training, Leland was transferred to Fort Devens, Massachusetts, where his music skills earned him a place in the 18th Army Band. For seven months, he played clarinet and saxophone at retirement ceremonies, holiday balls, and officer galas. Music became his breath between drills. The weight of war still hung in the air, but here, notes replaced gunfire, and harmonies replaced orders. He also served a brief rotation in the personnel office, typing rosters, updating assignment records, and learning the delicate machinery of Army logistics. His commanding officer noted, "Quiet. Diligent. Reliable. Exceptional mind for systems."

But across the ocean, the world was shifting.

On June 25, 1950, North Korea invaded the South, and the United States entered a war that would soon be called "forgotten." Leland, like so many others, received his deployment orders with little fanfare. He packed his duffel with standard-issue gear, a photograph

CHAPTER 3

THE BATTLE OF UNSAN

WHEN LELAND ARRIVED in Korea on August 6, 1950, the welcome was little more than heat, dust, and shouted orders. The ship that had carried him across the Pacific docked at Pusan Harbor under a white haze of diesel fumes and distant artillery. There were no bands, no banners—just the hollow clang of boots on metal ramps and the heavy knowledge that this wasn't training anymore.

He was assigned to K Company, 3rd Battalion, 8th Cavalry Regiment, part of the storied 1st Cavalry Division. The men had been fighting since the early days of the Pusan Perimeter—grinding battles against waves of North Korean troops, with heat like a hammer and supplies stretched thin. By the time Leland joined them, they were pushing north, lifted by the success of the Inchon Landing and the promise that the war might soon be over.

The terrain was cruel—jagged mountains, sudden fogs, and rivers that could flood without warning. The monsoon rains had turned the dirt roads to sucking mud, and the nights brought a cold that made every joint ache. Leland, now carrying the 40-pound Browning Automatic Rifle—nearly half his own body weight—never once complained. When asked if he wanted to swap for a lighter weapon, he shook his head. "This one works," he said. "And I know how to fix it."

His comrades took note. Leland was quiet, but not timid. He listened more than he spoke, asked questions when he didn't understand something, and moved with the cautious precision of a man who'd once taken apart toasters for fun. He kept his boots clean, his gear squared away, and his letters home folded neatly in his shirt pocket.

In the trenches and forward positions, Leland found flickers of camaraderie. He shared foxholes with a fiddle-playing kid from Kentucky and swapped stories with a sergeant who fed strays and quoted Hemingway. At night, he sometimes played his harmonica low and soft, barely louder than the wind. "Sounds like back home," someone whispered once.

But even in these brief moments of peace, the war hovered. Tension buzzed just beneath the surface like a wire ready to snap.

By late October, the 8th Cavalry had crossed into North Korea. General MacArthur confidently proclaimed the war would be over within days and the troops would be "Home by Christmas." The mood in camp was cautiously optimistic, the men passing cigarettes and counting the days. Leland didn't believe it. There was something in the air—something unspoken but sharp-edged. Rumors swirled of Chinese forces massing across the Yalu River, but MacArthur dismissed them as speculation.

Then came Unsan.

On the evening of November 1, K Company was stationed near a river crossing just outside the small village. The air had turned bitter. A low mist clung to the ground, and frost formed on the barrels of their rifles. Leland sat with his squad near a battered jeep, inspecting his weapon and tightening the strap on his helmet. There was an eerie stillness—no birdsong, no distant gunfire, just silence.

Then came the sound: a long, wavering echo of horns. Chinese bugles.

They came in waves. Tens of thousands of Chinese soldiers, fresh from the north, surged down the hills under cover of darkness. They moved with terrifying coordination, flanking the perimeter and severing communications in minutes. Explosions lit the horizon. The earth shook. Bullets tore through trees like needles through cloth.

K Company was surrounded.

Leland fired until his BAR overheated and jammed. Then he grabbed his e-tool and fought hand-to-hand. He pulled a wounded soldier from the open field, dragging him through mud and blood toward a collapsed wall. His leg burned—he'd been hit, but there was no time to stop. No time to think.

As the night dragged on, their ammunition dwindled. Radios were dead. Air support, promised and prayed for, never came—grounded by fog and Chinese anti-aircraft fire. They were alone.

By dawn on November 2, the surviving men were cold, exhausted, and encircled. Snow had begun to fall lightly, dusting the corpses of comrades and the husks of burned-out vehicles. Some tried to slip through the lines. Most were cut down.

Leland moved with a group attempting a breakout near a ravine. Gunfire erupted around them. Grenades arced through the smoke. He was hit again—this time in the ribs—and thrown against a twisted, blackened jeep. His breath caught. Blood soaked through his uniform, warm and slick. The pain was sharp and immediate. His vision blurred.

Through the ringing in his ears, he heard voices shouting. He tried to push himself up but collapsed. Somewhere in the fog, someone screamed his name. A medic? A friend? He didn't know.

Leland lay still, the cold seeping into his bones. His hand clutched at the harmonica in his pocket. He thought of home. He thought of 65 Plum Street and the porch in summer. He thought of Helen's face beneath the stars.

In his final moment of consciousness, he whispered, "Mom."

Then everything went black.

CHAPTER 4

A PRISONER'S ENDURANCE

When Leland awoke, he was flat on his back in the snow, staring into the barrel of a rifle and the eyes of a man who did not speak his language. A Chinese officer, wrapped in a tattered winter coat, barked orders in sharp Mandarin. Rough hands pulled Leland to his feet. Pain shot through his ribs and leg. His uniform was stiff with blood. His harmonica, somehow, was still in his pocket.

He had been captured.

The march began before sunrise. A long, broken line of prisoners staggered through the North Korean wilderness, guarded by soldiers whose expressions were carved from stone. The wounded limped or were carried. Some died where they fell. Leland refused to let go of the soldier beside him—PFC Martin, a kid from Illinois who had lost a boot and was barely conscious. For two days, Leland supported Martin's weight with one arm and used the other to steady his own steps. A guard raised a rifle in warning. Leland kept walking.

The guard spat in the snow and looked away.

Food was scarce. Some days, they were given nothing. On others, a small tin cup of watery millet porridge passed for a meal. Water was snow scooped from the roadside. The wind tore at their faces. Frostbite crept into fingers and toes. Each night, they collapsed into exhausted heaps on the frozen ground, huddled for warmth beneath rags and hope.

By mid-November, the march ended. They arrived at a makeshift camp deep in the mountains—no more than a collection of mud huts and dugouts built into the hillside. Barbed wire was strung between trees. There were no beds. No blankets. No heat. Just straw on packed earth and a silence so complete it pressed on the lungs.

This was not a prison. This was purgatory.

Disease spread like wildfire. Dysentery claimed the first victims, followed by pneumonia, typhus, and the slow wasting of starvation. Leland's frame, once lean and strong, began to wither. His belt notched tighter with each week. The rations—when they came—were barely enough to sustain breath.

Medical treatment was nonexistent. Wounds festered. Teeth fell out. Bodies failed. But in the darkness, Leland resisted the only way he could: by refusing to surrender his humanity.

He tore strips from his undershirt to bind infected cuts. He helped bury the dead with dignity, whispering their names into the frozen air. He sang—softly at first, then louder when others joined. He told stories of Bolivar, of Sunday dinners and sugar cones at the diner, of the maple tree at 65 Plum Street. He described Lady, his golden retriever, with such vivid detail that some prisoners began dreaming of her.

He organized nightly prayers—not religious sermons, just moments of reflection. Some nights, it was a Psalm. Other nights, a line of poetry or a Boy Scout oath. He and another prisoner—Corporal Anselmo, a carpenter from Pittsburgh—whittled a chess set from pine twigs and bottle caps. They played silently, their breath visible in the cold.

When Chinese officers ordered the prisoners to attend hours-long propaganda lectures, Leland sat quietly, eyes forward, refusing to nod or react. He trained himself not to flinch during interrogations. He gave only his name, rank, and serial number. His resolve became armor. His endurance, a quiet act of defiance.

her and pulled her into a long, silent embrace. There were no words. None were needed. She pressed her face against his neck, breathed in the scent of dust, metal, and the faintest trace of his cologne.

That night, the Sugar Bowl diner stayed open past midnight. The jukebox played swing tunes. Friends came and went, some laughing, some unable to speak. Leland sat at the corner booth, slowly sipping a vanilla malted, answering questions with a nod or a quiet "yes, ma'am." But his eyes were distant, watchful. Every loud noise made him flinch. Every sudden laugh seemed to echo too sharply.

For days, he hardly slept. The nights brought dreams—vivid, disjointed, and terrifying. He would wake gasping, tangled in sweat-drenched sheets, the cry of "Incoming!" still ringing in his ears. He once mistook the sound of firecrackers for artillery and dove instinctively to the floor. Belle never scolded. She just held him.

When a reporter from the Bolivar Breeze asked for an interview, Leland declined at first. But after a week, he agreed—on the condition that it be done at the church, alone, with no photos. He sat in the front pew of the Bolivar Methodist sanctuary, hands folded, voice low.

"I was captured on November 2nd," he said. "At Unsan. We were surrounded. No food. No radio. We fought until we couldn't. I was wounded and taken."

He paused, looked at the stained-glass window above the altar.

"I remember the cold more than anything. The kind that settles in your bones. But worse was the silence afterward. The waiting. The wondering if anyone would remember we were out there."

When the reporter asked him what kept him going, he answered without hesitation: "Bolivar. My family. And Helen. I had to come home."

The article ended with a quote from Leland's old Boy Scout handbook:

"Be prepared. And never forget the ones who aren't here."

The town clipped the piece and pinned it to bulletin boards, fridge doors, and church entrances. His story became legend. But for Leland, it was never about heroism. It was about survival. And now, it was about finding a way to live again—not just exist, but live.

And though it would take time, and patience, and love, he was ready to try.

CHAPTER 6

A NEW DREAM

IN THE WEEKS following his return, Leland Blakeslee existed somewhere between two worlds—the familiar rhythms of Bolivar and the haunting memories of war. He walked its streets like a man awakening from a long fever, recognizing every storefront, every face, yet feeling slightly detached, like a ghost inhabiting his own life.

At night, the dreams still came.

Some were vivid—the bitter cold of the prison camp, the weight of a rifle, the bugle call before the ambush. Others were more abstract: Lady barking from the porch, Helen slipping through his fingers, his mother's voice echoing down a corridor that never ended. He would wake in the dark, breath shallow, heart pounding, the sheets twisted around him like vines.

But during the day, Leland clung to routine. It anchored him.

He helped Merle patch the garage roof and repainted the white trim on 65 Plum Street. He walked Lady's replacement, a spry mutt named Ginger, through the backwoods trail behind the school. Belle made him soft-boiled eggs every morning, even when he wasn't hungry. Ronnie shadowed him like the boy he once was, asking questions, filling the silence.

And Helen—Helen stayed.

She never pried. Never asked him to talk about Korea unless he chose to. Instead, she sat beside him on the porch swing, hand in his, as they listened to the wind rustle the leaves of the big sugar maple. Sometimes she read aloud. Sometimes she hummed. Sometimes they just watched the sky turn to dusk.

It was Belle, one quiet morning, who finally said what he needed to hear.

"You're home now, son," she whispered, resting a hand on his shoulder. "You did what you had to do. But now it's time to live the life you fought for."

Those words struck something in him—a long-dormant ember. That afternoon, he found his high school diploma and letters from his former teachers, tucked in a manila envelope in the chest under his bed. He flipped through the pages, pausing at the one from Mr. Renshaw, his science instructor: "You have a mind built for discovery. Don't let the world waste it."

That fall, Leland applied to college.

With help from the G.I. Bill, glowing recommendations, and a heartfelt essay about his dream to build a better world, he was accepted to Cornell University's College of Engineering. When the letter came, Helen read it aloud three times before Leland could believe it. Belle cried. Merle, ever a man of few words, simply nodded and said, "Knew you would."

Leland moved to Ithaca in January 1954, taking up residence in a modest dorm room with cinderblock walls, a twin bed, and a wooden desk just wide enough for a drafting board. He brought with him three things: a small suitcase, the photograph of Helen he'd carried through Korea, and his harmonica.

Cornell was a world apart. The campus buzzed with youthful ambition. Most of his classmates were younger—fresh-faced boys just out of high school. Leland, now 22, felt older in every way. But he didn't mind. He wasn't there for parties or prestige. He was there to work.

He majored in materials science and engineering, drawn by his childhood fascination with metals, machines, and the invisible forces that governed them. He excelled in thermodynamics, fluid dynamics, electrochemistry, and solid-state physics. His professors quickly noticed his work ethic and his eye for systems others overlooked.

He kept to himself at first, spending long hours in the engineering labs, soldering circuits, sketching blueprints, and running experiments that often failed before they succeeded. But slowly, a small circle formed around him—other veterans, curious students, and professors intrigued by his unconventional ideas and gentle persistence.

It was during his junior year that Leland heard a lecture that changed everything.

The guest speaker was a visiting scientist from Bell Labs, discussing hydrogen—its properties, abundance, and untapped potential as a clean energy source. As he spoke about fuel cells—devices that could convert hydrogen into electricity with only water and heat as byproducts—Leland's pen slowed. His mind raced.

He remembered Bolivar. The layoffs at Sinclair Oil. The way Merle had once come home, hat in hand, not knowing if he'd be working the next week. He remembered the soot-black snow, the broken-down furnaces, the homes lit by kerosene lanterns during outages.

He thought, What if we could build something better?

That night, Leland stayed in the lab until 3 a.m., sketching ideas on the back of an old exam booklet. A portable fuel cell. No emissions. No noise. Just clean, steady power.

For his senior project, he built it.

He spent months refining the design—scavenging parts from discarded lab equipment, experimenting with different membranes, adjusting pressures and catalysts. He lived on coffee, peanut butter crackers, and sheer will.

On a cold March morning in 1958, Leland flipped the final

switch. A row of lightbulbs flickered to life, powered solely by his device. There was no smoke. No hum. Just soft, clean light.

He wept.

His invention earned him the Edison Award for Innovation, the university's highest honor for undergraduate engineering. At graduation, he walked across the stage to a standing ovation, graduating summa cum laude with the dean of engineering shaking his hand and saying, "You're going to change the world, Mr. Blakeslee."

And the very next day, he did something even greater.

He married Helen.

The wedding was held at the Bolivar Methodist Church, beneath the same steeple where he once rang the bell as a boy. The sanctuary was filled to the rafters—family, friends, veterans, neighbors, and strangers who had read his story in the Breeze and felt like they knew him. Belle wore blue and wept throughout. Merle smiled wider than anyone had seen in years.

Ronnie played drums at the reception with his high school band, The Geysers. Barbara sang a solo. Helen wore her mother's lace gown and carried lilies of the valley.

That night, as the stars emerged over the hills, Leland stood on the porch of the Bolivar Hotel, his arm around his wife, and whispered:

"This is the life I fought for."

And she replied, "Then let's build it—together."

CHAPTER 8

BLAKESLEE ENERGY

By 1970, LELAND Blakeslee had achieved more than most men dare to imagine. His work had helped power mankind to the moon. He was respected in scientific circles, known as a man of quiet brilliance and uncompromising integrity. He had a family he adored, a modest house in a Cleveland suburb, and a job at NASA that would have kept him comfortable for life.

But Leland was not interested in comfort.

Space had always been a marvel—but Earth was his mission.

Even as he watched astronauts walk the lunar surface, he couldn't stop thinking about homes like 65 Plum Street, where winters were cold and fuel was unreliable. He thought about small towns and farmsteads with sputtering furnaces and outages that plunged entire neighborhoods into darkness. He thought about families who still boiled water over kerosene stoves and children who read by candlelight when the grid failed.

And he began to ask a question that had haunted him since Cornell:

What if every home could make its own power—cleanly, quietly, affordably?

That same year, Leland made a bold decision. He left NASA.

It surprised many. General Electric had already made him an offer, and in Niskayuna, New York, he found what he needed: resources, labs, and a team of brilliant minds ready to push the limits of fuel cell technology for civilian use.

At GE, he led development on early home-scale hydrogen systems. The work was groundbreaking—but slow. Corporate bureaucracy weighed heavily. Promising prototypes were shelved due to market hesitation. Executives hesitated at the notion of decentralizing energy.

Leland grew restless.

In 1978, at age forty-seven, he walked away from GE, turned down a lucrative counteroffer, and returned home to Bolivar.

He didn't go alone.

Ronnie—now a seasoned electrician and machinist—met him at The Sugar Bowl with a wide grin and an open truck bed full of salvaged parts. The brothers hadn't worked side by side since they were boys, but they fell back into rhythm as if no time had passed.

They set up shop in the garage behind 65 Plum Street, the same one where Lady had once watched their childhood experiments. The floor was oil-stained. The light was dim. The tools were mismatched and mostly secondhand. But for Leland, it was perfect.

They called their fledgling company Blakeslee Energy.

Their mission: to design and build a hydrogen fuel cell system that could power a single home—reliably, safely, and cheaply.

They started with nothing but an idea, a soldering iron, and a dream.

The first prototype was clunky—an eyesore of valves, wires, and hissing pressure regulators. But it worked. It powered a lightbulb, then a fan, then a full room. They named it Lady I, in honor of their long-gone retriever. Her name was etched in brass on the side panel.

Word spread quickly. Engineers from Rochester and Buffalo drove down to see it. Articles appeared in the Wellsville Daily Reporter, then in the Buffalo News. By 1980, they had hired their first employees—local welders, machinists, and former classmates who remembered Leland from his high school days.

They moved from the garage to a warehouse on the edge of town. Then a second. Then a third.

By 1985, Blakeslee Energy employed over 4,000 people and shipped fuel cell units across the country.

Their flagship product—the Blakeslee Box—was compact, efficient, and revolutionary. It generated electricity using hydrogen and oxygen, emitting only water vapor and warmth. With no moving parts and minimal maintenance, it was ideal for rural homes, remote clinics, and disaster-prone regions. For the first time, families without access to reliable power had a new option.

Leland refused to patent parts that could save lives. He released dozens of core designs to the public domain, ensuring that nonprofits, hospitals, and even competitors could build upon his work. His philosophy was simple:

"The light should belong to everyone."

When asked what drove his relentless innovation, Leland always pointed back to Bolivar. "I wanted to make something that would help towns like mine," he told a Popular Mechanics interviewer. "Something that says, you don't have to leave home to build a better future."

He rarely gave interviews, declined television appearances, and turned down offers to take the company public. He wore plain suits, traveled coach, and still carried his harmonica in his breast pocket.

At industry conferences, he could be found sitting in the back row, scribbling notes in the margins of brochures. When introduced on stage, he nodded politely and returned humbly to his seat.

He didn't want fame.

He wanted impact.

CHAPTER 9

THE SEEDS OF HOPE

BY THE LATE 1980s, Blakeslee Energy was no longer just a company—it was a movement.

Leland had achieved what many thought impossible: clean, decentralized power in a box no larger than a washing machine. The Blakeslee Box had transformed lives in rural Montana and hurricane-ravaged Louisiana. It powered cabins in the Adirondacks, health clinics in Appalachia, and Navajo homes long overlooked by the grid. The units ran quietly, needed almost no maintenance, and could keep a family warm in winter or a refrigerator running in a blackout. Word of mouth had made them legendary.

But Leland's vision reached farther than the U.S. power grid. He began asking himself the same question he had asked years before:

What if the light could go farther still?

It began with a letter from a schoolteacher in Malawi. Her name was Grace. She had read about the Blakeslee Box in an international engineering journal and asked if it was true—that such a thing could power a classroom where the sun set before homework was done.

Leland sent her one—free of charge.

He included a note: "For your students. May their future be brighter than our past."

She wrote back months later. Her students were now studying at night and the small clinic next door had light for delivering babies. They no longer feared the dark.

Leland wept quietly when he read it.

In 1988, he founded a nonprofit division of the company and named it after the place where it all began: 65Plum.

Its mission was radical in its simplicity: for every ten Blakeslee Boxes sold commercially, one would be donated—no strings, no catch—to a family, clinic, or school in a developing nation.

From the first shipment, the impact was immediate.

In Uganda, midwives told stories of delivering babies with flashlights—until the Blakeslee Box gave them real, reliable light. In Peru, coffee farmers used it to power bean dryers, cutting spoilage in half. In Cambodia, students gathered under new electric bulbs and took their national exams for the first time under proper lighting.

Leland personally visited over two dozen countries. He preferred the back of the plane, carried his own bags, and always stayed with locals. He sat cross-legged in huts and under open skies, listening to stories translated between languages and smiles. He took notes. He asked questions. He adjusted his designs for dusty roads, monsoon rains, and places where tools were few but hope was boundless.

In every village, he brought a gift: not just power, but dignity.

The demand for Blakeslee Boxes surged across the Global South. Aid organizations took notice. Governments called. But Leland held to his one unwavering rule:

Only democratic nations could receive them.

Not because he played politics, but because he believed freedom and light were intertwined.

"You can't empower people," he said once, "if you don't first give them the power to turn on a light—and the freedom to speak beneath it, worship beside it, dream beyond it, and live without fear within it.

By 1998, the company reached a milestone few thought possible: 100 million units distributed across 74 democratic nations.

That same year, Leland stepped down as CEO.

Not because he was tired, but because it was time.

He passed the mantle to his daughter, Jacqueline Lee Blakeslee—Jackie—who had grown up in the hum of machines and the glow of soldering irons. She had earned her MBA from St. Bonaventure University, interned with Engineers Without Borders, and risen through the company ranks not as a legacy hire, but as a force of nature.

At 32, she became the youngest female CEO of a multinational energy company.

In her first public address, Jackie stood before a crowd of employees in the Bolivar plant and said, "My father taught me that invention means nothing without intention. He built this company not to profit, but to serve. I promise to do the same."

And she did.

Under her leadership, Blakeslee Energy diversified its offerings. They introduced solar and wind hybrid add-ons. They created energy storage solutions for regions with inconsistent sun or wind. They developed new medical-grade fuel cells for mobile clinics and disaster relief. The company stayed private, stayed lean, and stayed true to its founding principles.

Meanwhile, Leland retreated from the day-to-day operations.

He didn't retire—he simply reoriented.

Because once again, the questions in his mind had shifted. He had brought light to homes and hope to towns. But there were still shadows in the world he couldn't ignore. Shadows that no machine could fix.

So he asked again:

What if…

CHAPTER 10

IT'S KIND OF FUN TO DO THE IMPOSSIBLE

BY THE DAWN of the new millennium, Leland Blakeslee had built not just machines, but movements.

He lit up villages, transformed small towns, and turned a childhood dream into a global legacy. Yet in the stillness of his later years—in the quiet moments when the house was dark and the wind-swept gently across the Bolivar hills—his mind turned inward.

Leland saw larger systems that left too many behind—through both cruelty and inertia. He believed America had both the means and the mandate to do better.

And so, nearing seventy, Leland turned his attention to two of the most formidable issues of his time: retirement and healthcare.

He started with retirement—haunted, perhaps, by the sight of Merle and Belle counting coins in the final years of their lives, uncertain if their Social Security would last the month.

He asked:

What if every American could retire in dignity, as a millionaire—not through luck or markets, but by birthright?

He proposed a radical but mathematically sound system. At birth,

37

every American would receive $50,000 deposited into a federally managed, interest-bearing account, invested in ultra-secure government bonds with a fixed annual return of 6%.

No risk. No speculation. No middlemen.

The principal couldn't be touched until age 60. The funds would be tax-free. Individuals could voluntarily contribute more, but no one would ever lose what they hadn't gambled. Upon death, the balance would pass to designated heirs.

His projections stunned economists:

At age 60: $1.81 million

At age 65: $2.45 million

At age 70: $3.29 million

He published white papers. He gave university lectures. He sat with skeptical lawmakers, ran the numbers, answered their doubts.

Some said it was impossible. Leland smiled and replied, "So was the moon."

To jump-start the vision, he pledged $1 billion of his own fortune—enough to seed 20,000 accounts for newborns in underserved communities. By the end of the first year, other philanthropists had joined him. A movement had begun.

But he wasn't finished.

Next, he turned to healthcare.

He remembered the battered soldiers of Unsan. The frail children he'd seen in Appalachian clinics. The single mothers throughout America juggling three part-time jobs and still afraid of getting sick. He saw a system not built to heal, but to bill.

So he asked:

What if healthcare were a right, not a privilege?

He proposed a single-payer system modeled after Medicare, expanded to cover every citizen. No deductibles. No premiums. No co-pays. Just a simple card that said: You matter. You're covered.

Funding would come from a fair-share tax system—those who

A year later, he made a quiet donation to the hospital—enough to help fund a new Neonatal Intensive Care Unit, one of the first of its kind in the region. He never spoke publicly about it, never asked that his name be attached. But the wing opened in 1966, and in small letters on the donor plaque outside the entrance, it read:

"For the tiny lights the night could not dim." — L.B.

Meanwhile, his work at NASA advanced.

By 1965, Leland's team had finalized the fuel cell system for the Gemini program. The cells were smaller, lighter, and more reliable than anyone had hoped. They powered cabin systems, communication equipment, and onboard computers—cleanly, quietly, and efficiently.

Then came Apollo.

Leland's fuel cell designs formed the backbone of the electrical systems for the Apollo Command Module. The cells were critical—without them, there would be no lights, no telemetry, no air.

He knew what was at stake.

He watched each launch with a mix of pride and nerves. He sat with Helen and Jackie, now five, as they gathered around the black-and-white television in their living room, breath held each time a countdown reached zero.

And then, on July 20, 1969, Leland watched history unfold.

Neil Armstrong's voice crackled through the speaker: "That's one small step for man, one giant leap for mankind."

Leland sat on the couch, Jackie curled in his lap, Helen beside him. His eyes welled with tears—not just for the moon, but for the journey that had led there: from a garage in Bolivar to a POW camp in Korea to this singular moment when human ingenuity reached beyond Earth.

He didn't say a word.

He just held his daughter close.

CHAPTER 7

FROM EARTH TO THE MOON

AFTER THEIR WEDDING, Leland and Helen moved into a modest brick apartment on the edge of Ithaca, close enough for Leland to bike to the Cornell campus while finishing a brief research fellowship. They bought secondhand furniture from a retired professor, a hand-me-down phonograph from Barbara, and filled the shelves with books—textbooks, poetry, and a growing collection of engineering journals that Leland read like scripture.

But by the spring of 1959, opportunity came knocking from far beyond the hills of Western New York.

NASA—newly formed and racing against the Soviet Union toward the stars—had been scouting young engineers with cutting-edge ideas in alternative power systems. Leland's fuel cell prototype, already generating buzz in academic circles, had found its way into the hands of a senior engineer at NASA's Lewis Research Center in Brook Park, Ohio.

An offer followed: join a classified research division exploring the use of hydrogen fuel cells in manned spacecraft.

Leland accepted without hesitation.

He and Helen packed their belongings into a small U-Haul, said tearful goodbyes to their families in Bolivar, and drove west toward Cleveland—toward the unknown.

The Lewis Research Center was a temple of innovation, buzzing with minds set on the impossible. Leland stepped into that world with quiet awe. Inside the labs were men and women who had once built bombers, satellites, and rocket engines, now harnessing their intellect to solve the challenges of spaceflight: zero gravity, life support, thermal extremes, and above all, reliable power.

The Apollo program had just begun.

Leland joined a small, elite team working on spacecraft power systems. His focus: make fuel cells compact, efficient, and failproof. The devices needed to operate in vacuum, withstand violent launches, and function with no room for error. Every ounce mattered. Every watt counted.

He thrived in the pressure.

He worked long hours under fluorescent lights, hunched over circuit boards and cooling systems, testing membranes and catalysts. He redesigned heat exchangers, developed new insulation coatings, and helped troubleshoot critical problems in early prototypes that overheated or lost pressure under stress.

His colleagues learned quickly that Leland was a man of few words and absolute integrity. He documented everything meticulously, never took shortcuts, and asked the right questions at the right moments. When others gave up on a malfunctioning component, Leland stayed behind with a soldering iron, tinkering into the early hours.

In 1963, Leland and Helen welcomed their daughter, Jacqueline Lee Blakeslee—named for Jackie Kennedy and Helen's great-grandmother. Jackie was born at Rainbow Babies & Children's Hospital in Cleveland, three weeks premature but healthy. Leland held her for the first time with trembling hands, overwhelmed by the simple miracle of a new life.

impossibly, there. Belle let out a sound somewhere between a sob and a scream. She rushed to him, arms outstretched, tears already spilling down her cheeks. "My boy! My sweet boy!" she cried, folding him into her embrace, her fingers clutching the fabric of his shirt like she might anchor him to life itself.

Merle stood frozen for a moment, blinking as though trying to wake from a dream. Then he stepped forward and wrapped them both in his arms. For the first time in his life, he wept openly.

Within minutes, the word spread. Church bells rang without warning. The Bolivar Breeze rushed out a bulletin. Children on bicycles tore down the streets shouting, "Leland's home! Leland's home!"

Neighbors flooded the yard. Mrs. Hartley from next door brought a pie. Reverend Gilmore arrived with a prayer. Even old Mr. Collins, who hadn't left his porch in years, shuffled down the sidewalk to shake Leland's hand.

The town rallied with a spontaneity that only deep love can summon. A parade was organized by dusk. Red, white, and blue bunting materialized along Main Street. The Bolivar Central marching band reassembled—many still in summer clothes—dusting off drums and horns in the back of the school auditorium. The mayor, hoisting a borrowed megaphone, declared, "Today, Bolivar welcomes home its son!"

Leland rode down Main Street in a gleaming red 1953 Ford Crestline convertible, loaned by Ferris & Forbes Ford. He wore a borrowed suit that hung slightly loose on his frame. Ronnie, now taller and leaner, jogged alongside the car with one hand on the door.

Helen stood near the Methodist Church steps, her arms pressed tightly to her sides, heart pounding. She had imagined this moment a thousand different ways, in dreams and prayers. But nothing prepared her for the reality of him.

When their eyes met, Leland raised a hand, then stepped down from the car, ignoring the calls of the crowd. He walked directly to

CHAPTER 5

THE HOMECOMING

IT WAS A humid afternoon in late August 1953 when a dark green Army staff car rolled slowly down Plum Street, its white-wall tires crunching softly against the gravel shoulder. The crickets fell silent. Curtains stirred. At number 65, Belle Blakeslee stood in the doorway, apron still dusted with flour, her hands cradling a dishtowel. She had just pulled a cherry pie from the oven and was humming a hymn when the sedan came to a stop.

Two men in uniform stepped out.

Her breath caught in her throat. The towel slipped from her fingers. Her knees went weak.

"Merle," she called out, barely a whisper. "It's them."

He was already behind her, wiping his hands on a Sinclair Oil rag. When he saw the car, he moved instinctively, catching Belle as she sagged toward the floor, her voice trembling: "No... no, not again..."

But the officers did not approach with solemn expressions or folded papers.

They turned, stepped aside—and revealed him.

Leland.

Alive.

Pale, thin, hair shorn close and eyes sunken, but unmistakably,

Christmas 1950 passed like a shadow. There were no decorations, no gifts—only the faint echo of a carol. Leland recited the nativity story from memory. He hummed "Silent Night" into the cold, cracked air. Others joined, their voices weak but unwavering. For a moment, it felt like a sanctuary.

The seasons blurred into each other. Three years passed like smoke. Spring brought mud and mosquitos. Summer brought rot. Winter, death. Yet through it all, Leland survived. Barely. But completely.

When the armistice was signed in July 1953, and word of prisoner exchanges finally reached the camp, many wept openly. Some didn't believe it. Others had been prisoners so long they no longer remembered how to hope.

But on a morning in early August, trucks arrived. Uniformed medics appeared. American flags were unfurled. And for the first time in over a thousand days, Leland saw the Stars and Stripes.

He weighed 95 pounds. His eyes were sunken, his gait unsteady. But when a nurse handed him a clipboard and asked him to state his name, he straightened and said, "Leland Blakeslee. Bolivar, New York."

He was flown to a hospital in Tokyo for emergency care. Doctors examined his X-rays and marveled at his survival. "Sheer willpower," one said.

When Leland was finally handed a pencil and paper, he wrote a single letter—his handwriting shaky but unmistakable:

August 12, 1953

Dear Mom and Dad,

I'm alive. I'll be home soon.

Please tell Helen.

Love,

Leland

of Helen, the small black Bible his mother had given him at Christmas, and his harmonica—scratched, dented, and still in tune.

His final letter from American soil was written on Army stationery from a base in San Francisco. It arrived in Bolivar five days after he boarded the ship:

August 1, 1950

Dear Mom and Dad,

By the time you read this, I'll be out at sea.

I don't know what's ahead, but I trust I'm on the right path. There's a reason I'm going. I can feel it. I carry you both with me every step of the way. Please give Lady a pat from me, and tell Helen I'll write when I can.

Love,

Leland

Helen cried when she read it. Belle didn't. She folded the letter, placed it in the box with the others, and lit a candle beneath the framed photograph of Leland in his pressed uniform. She would keep it burning until he came home.

At sea, Leland stared at the horizon each night, his fingers brushing the edges of his harmonica. The Pacific seemed endless, but his mind stayed fixed on home: on the scent of maple leaves in October, on Helen's laughter echoing off the canyon walls of Letchworth, on his mother's humming while she kneaded bread.

He had no illusions. He knew where he was going. But he also knew who he was.

And that, he believed, might be enough.

had more would pay more. Leland believed that to whom much is given, much is expected—and generosity was a form of patriotism. He believed prevention was cheaper than emergency. He believed paperwork didn't cure people—compassion did.

When he presented his ideas before Congress, he carried with him a worn copy of Franklin Delano Roosevelt's Four Freedoms speech. He placed it on the podium and read aloud:

Freedom of speech

Freedom of worship

Freedom from want

Freedom from fear

Then he added:

"These freedoms are not sentimental relics. They are not optional. And they are not possible without security in old age, in health, and in the knowledge that we are seen—not as numbers but as neighbors."

He looked every lawmaker in the eye, as if daring them to believe.

And in the silence that followed, many did.

But even as he helped solve the formidable issues of retirement and healthcare, there were shadows still.

He thought of the soldiers he had left behind at Unsan. He thought of the survivors—men who came home but never truly returned. He thought of the tired eyes he'd seen at VA hospitals, the names etched into stone in towns across America, the stories never told because silence had become their shelter.

And so he asked the question that had become his compass:

What if?

What if veterans could come home not just to parades—but to peace?

With support from the 65Plum Foundation, Leland broke ground on his most personal project yet: The Belle Blakeslee Veterans Haven, named for his mother, who had waited by the window for letters during three long winters.

The facility, nestled in the green hills outside Olean, New York, was unlike anything the country had seen.

It was not a hospital. It was not a shelter.

It was a home.

There were no waiting rooms with flickering televisions. No sterile white walls. No cold, bureaucratic voices behind glass. Instead, there were counselors, chefs, therapy dogs, music rooms, organic gardens, and classrooms. There were art studios and hiking trails, family cottages and career centers. There was dignity.

The Haven offered full-spectrum care: mental health counseling, trauma-informed therapy, substance recovery, housing, job training, family reintegration, and above all—community. No veteran ever received a bill.

Leland personally welcomed the first group of residents. Many were as young as he had been at Unsan. Some wore their wounds visibly. Others, silently.

He shook their hands, looked them in the eye, and said, "You're home now. Let's rebuild together."

CHAPTER 11

A PLACE TO REST

THE RIBBON-CUTTING CEREMONY for The Belle Blakeslee Veterans Haven was held on a crisp September morning. The sun shone brilliantly on the hills outside Olean, casting long golden streaks across the freshly mown lawn and the polished brass nameplate at the entryway.

Leland stood at the podium, shoulders slightly stooped now, hair mostly silver, but eyes clear and steady as ever. Beside him stood Helen, elegant in a midnight blue coat, her gloved hand wrapped gently around his arm. Jackie was there too, with her own daughter on her hip—Leland's first grandchild—watching her grandfather with eyes full of awe.

Veterans had come from every corner of the country. Some wore ribbons from Vietnam, others the desert dust of the Persian Gulf. Still others wore only the deep, quiet lines of trauma etched in their faces. They stood with heads bowed as Leland spoke.

"I was once a boy who came home broken," he said, his voice quiet but carrying. "This place is for those who didn't know if they'd ever be whole again. May you find healing here. And light."

With those words, he cut the ribbon. The crowd applauded.

Cameras clicked. Somewhere, a child released a red balloon and it rose into the bright blue sky like a benediction.

Later that afternoon, Leland and Helen began the drive back to Bolivar taking the long way through the beautiful Finger Lakes. The route wound through the familiar hills of Allegany County—past the sugar maples, the old Sinclair plant, the trails he once hiked as a boy. The car was quiet. Helen played soft music on the radio. Leland's hand rested on hers atop the gearshift.

An hour into the drive, just past a scenic overlook near Keuka Lake, Leland spoke.

"Pull over for a moment?"

Helen glanced at him, alarmed by the strain in his voice. She eased the car onto the gravel shoulder.

"I just need some air," he said.

They stepped out. The view stretched wide—rolling farmland, treetops beginning to blush with early autumn, the lake shimmering far below. A cool breeze lifted the collar of his coat. Leland walked slowly to a wooden bench and sat. He stared out at the valley, breathing deeply, as if committing it all to memory.

Helen joined him, concerned. "Are you alright?"

He nodded, then looked at her—not with fear, but with purpose.

"If I don't make it home," he said gently, "promise me something."

"Leland…"

"Promise me you'll take care of the boys. The boys of Unsan. And all the others. Keep the lights on for them."

Helen gripped his hand tightly. "Don't say that."

But he didn't answer right away. He simply looked out over the land he loved, the sky he had helped others reach, the world he had tried so hard to improve.

Then he exhaled—and didn't inhale again.

His grip loosened in hers.

Helen held him and cried out his name, again and again, as the wind rustled through the leaves, as if the earth itself were taking a deep breath in his place.

News of Leland Blakeslee's death swept through Bolivar and beyond like thunder and lightning giving way to quiet light.

The President issued a statement of condolence. NASA released a commemorative video highlighting his contributions to the Apollo missions. Newspapers across the country ran tributes, calling him The Man Who Lit the World.

Flags flew at half-mast throughout Allegany County. Churches held vigils. Schoolchildren drew pictures of lightbulbs and stars and fuel cells and mailed them to the Blakeslee family. Jackie received over 7,000 letters—some from scientists, some from world leaders, most from ordinary people whose lives had been illuminated, literally or figuratively, by her father's work.

The funeral was held at the Bolivar Methodist Church, where Leland had once rung the bell as a boy. The sanctuary was filled with engineers, veterans, teachers, and former POWs who owed their lives to a man who never stopped asking what if.

Jackie delivered the eulogy.

"My father believed in possibility," she said, standing behind the same pulpit where he had once spoken as a teenager. "He believed that light could change lives. But more than that, he believed in kindness. He believed in quiet work, in second chances, in dignity, and in building things that outlive us. His inventions lit up homes. But his greatest creation was hope."

He was buried beneath an oak tree in Maple Lawn Cemetery, just a few miles from 65 Plum Street. The same cemetery where Belle and Merle rested. The same land where he once raced soapbox cars with Ronnie and fixed radios in the garage.

His headstone was simple, made of dark granite.

It read:

Leland Blakeslee

1931–2005

What if...

CHAPTER 12

THE PORCH

THE YEAR IS 1950.

The leaves on the big sugar maple at 65 Plum Street have begun to turn—their edges dipped in amber and fire. The air smells of burning wood, of cinnamon from a pie cooling on the kitchen windowsill. Bolivar is quiet, settling into its long exhale before winter.

Inside the house, Belle Blakeslee is ironing shirts when the knock comes.

It is soft, polite, the way only official knocks seem to be.

She walks to the door slowly, heart pounding, towel still in hand. Through the lace curtain, she sees them: a chaplain in dress uniform, a young officer holding a folded paper in one hand, a hat pressed against his chest with the other.

"No," she whispers.

The towel drops.

Her knees buckle.

Merle catches her just before she hits the floor.

They don't have to say it. They don't even get the words out. The air has changed. The world has shifted.

Leland Blakeslee, age nineteen, has been killed in action near Unsan, North Korea. Body not recovered. Presumed dead.

The chaplain reads his name.

Belle doesn't hear it.

She is far away now—somewhere between dream and memory.

In her mind, the door opens again—but this time, he's there. Thin, trembling, but alive. She throws her arms around him. The town erupts in celebration. The church bells ring. There's a parade down Main Street. Helen is waiting at the curb, waving through tears. Leland steps off the convertible and kisses her in front of the entire town. They marry. They have a daughter named Jackie. He works for NASA. He helps land men on the moon. He invents a little box that brings power to the powerless. He builds a company. A movement. A better world.

He saves lives.

He grows old beside Helen.

And when he dies, it is not in a trench, alone and bleeding—but in her arms, overlooking the hills that raised him.

In this vision, he lives.

Not just survives—lives.

Belle stirs on the floor of the living room.

Her head is in Merle's lap now. He strokes her hair, silently rocking her the way he once rocked his children after nightmares. She opens her eyes slowly. The room comes into focus.

"I saw him," she says faintly. "I saw everything. He built a whole life."

Merle doesn't know what to say. He just nods, his face tight with grief.

"He helped so many people," she whispers. "He married Helen. They had a little girl. He lit up the world."

She closes her eyes again, and a tear slips down her cheek.

"My boy," she murmurs. "He was a good man."

Outside, the wind stirs the leaves. The maple tree sways gently. Somewhere, a dog barks. The world keeps turning.

And in Belle's heart, in the place between sorrow and grace, she holds a single, sacred truth:

He could have lived.

He should have lived.

And if he had—

It would have been a wonderful life.

EPILOGUE

WHAT IF...

WHAT IF WAR had not stolen so many?

What if the knock on the door had never come?

What if a boy from 65 Plum Street had lived to marry the girl next door, raise a daughter, and light the world—not with bombs or bullets, but with hydrogen, hope, and unshakable faith in human goodness?

What if genius had not been buried beneath snow and silence, but given room to breathe, to build, to belong?

What if the world we live in is only a shadow of the one we could have made—had we chosen mercy over might, invention over destruction, dignity over despair?

What if every child, in every town, were given the chance to become not just who they are—but who they could have been?

Leland Blakeslee never lived to see his twentieth birthday.

Not in this world.

In this world, he died on a ridge near Unsan, in the cold, calling out for his mother. A name, a number, a telegram. One of thousands.

But in another world—a world built not on history, but on hope—he came home.

He healed. He loved. He dreamed.

He rebuilt. He reached. He remembered.

He changed the world—not with noise, but with light.

That imagined life, though never lived, still matters. Because it reminds us what is possible. What is worth fighting for. What is lost each time we send our sons to war, and each time we fail to ask the question he asked again and again:

What if?

What if we believed in something better?

What if we built it?

What if we remembered that behind every uniform is a porch, a promise, a family, a future?

What if...

Because in that question lives all the love we did not get to give, all the work we did not get to finish, all the beauty that might have been.

And because of that—because of him—we will never stop asking that question.

It would have been a wonderful life.

ABOUT THE AUTHOR

Shane Blakeslee is a husband, father, brother and entrepreneur. He is the founder of Blakeslee Technologies, an engineering and manufacturing firm. From Olean, New York, and now based in Cary, North Carolina, he also owns OriginalLIFEmagazines.com—the world's largest retailer of original LIFE magazines.

His debut novel, *Leland*, reimagines the life of a young man lost in the Korean War and explores the legacy he might have left behind. Inspired by personal history and a deep reverence for unrealized potential, Shane writes to honor the overlooked, the forgotten, and the futures cut short by war. His work asks the timeless question: What if?

THE UNSAN MEMORIAL:
THE BATTLE OF UNSAN, NOV. 1950

At Unsan, They Stood

Roll Call of U.S. Army Casualties — November 1-2, 1950

Between November 1 and 2, 1950, during the early stages of the Korean War, soldiers of the U.S. Army's 1st Cavalry Division—particularly the 3rd Battalion of the 8th Cavalry Regiment—came under heavy assault near the North Korean town of Unsan.

K Company was positioned on the northernmost flank, holding a forward defensive perimeter with limited support and supplies. They were attacked by elements of the Chinese People's Volunteer Army, whose arrival in the war had not yet been confirmed by U.S. intelligence. The Americans were outnumbered, isolated, and ultimately overwhelmed.

In just 48 hours, the regiment suffered catastrophic losses. An estimated 1,149 soldiers were killed, wounded, captured, or went missing. Many were young infantrymen on their first deployment. Few had time to retreat.

One of the men lost in the battle was Sergeant Leland Blakeslee, a 19-year-old from Western New York. This book imagines the life he might have lived. The section that follows honors those who didn't get that chance.

It is a list of names—by no means complete—but each represents a life given in service.

Each is part of the story of Unsan.

This is their roll call.

DONALD R ABEL
PVT US ARMY

FRANCIS H ABELE
SFC US ARMY

PHILIP W ACKLEY
PFC US ARMY

RONALD H ADAMS
CPL US ARMY

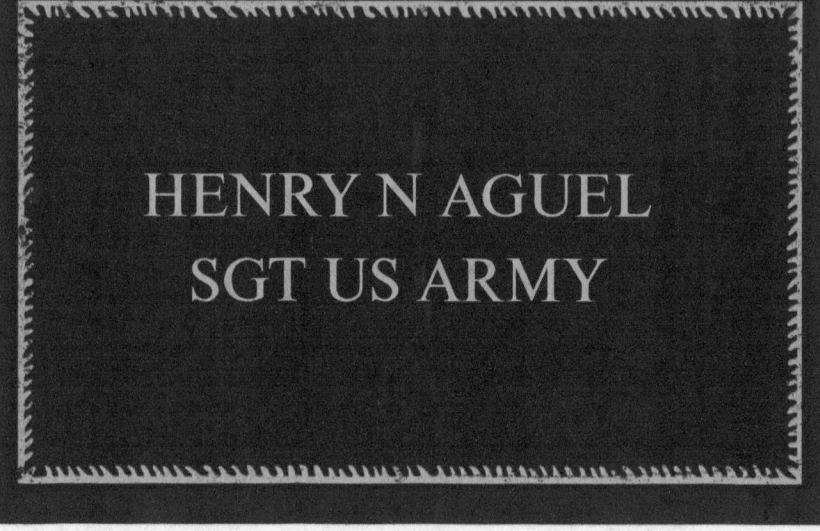

BILLIE F ADAMS
SGT US ARMY

HENRY N AGUEL
SGT US ARMY

BOBBY E AKERS
CPL US ARMY

W T AKINS
SFC US ARMY

JAMES A ALDERDICE
SGT US ARMY

HOWARD E ALEXANDER
PFC US ARMY

ALFRED H ALONZO
M/SGT US ARMY

WILLIAM H AMES
CPL US ARMY

CHARLES ARCE
CPL US ARMY

RICHARD J
ARCHAMBEAULT
SGT US ARMY

STANLEY P ARENDT
CPL US ARMY

BEVERLY I ARNOLD
CPL US ARMY

RECIL P ARWOOD
CPL US ARMY

DONALD L BAKIE
CPL US ARMY

JOSE BALALONG
SGT US ARMY

PASTOR BALANON
CPL US ARMY

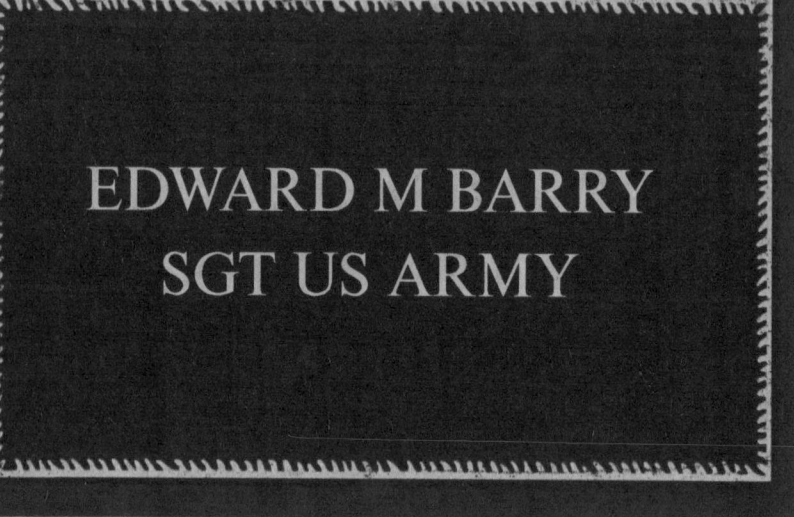

IVEY G BARNETT
PFC US ARMY

EDWARD M BARRY
SGT US ARMY

DAVEY H BART
CPL US ARMY

STANLEY E BAYLOR
SGT US ARMY

ALFRED BEAUCHESNE
M/SGT US ARMY

WILLIAM L BENGTSON
1ST LT US ARMY

NORMAN E BENSINGER
CPL US ARMY

ANTHONY BERNOSKY
SGT US ARMY

ROBERT H BERRY
CPL US ARMY

DONALD G BIAS
CPL US ARMY

LELAND F BLAKESLEE
SGT US ARMY

EDWARD F
BLAZEJEWSKI
CPL US ARMY

JOHN W BOBBS
SGT US ARMY

BRUCE D BOETTCHER
CPL US ARMY

WILLIAM N BONNER
CPL US ARMY

CLEM R BOODY
CPL US ARMY

ROLAND L BOWSER
PFC US ARMY

ULYSSES H BRADFORD
CAPT US ARMY

ELDON R BRADLEY
CPL US ARMY

FRANCIS BRAMANDE
SGT US ARMY

WILLIAM E BRASHEAR
SGT US ARMY

LLOYD K BROOKS
CPL US ARMY

HERMAN L BROTHERS
M/SGT US ARMY

CHARLES J BROWN
MSG US ARMY

ELGIE D BROWN
CPL US ARMY

ROBERT E BROWN
CPL US ARMY

RICHARD A BRYAN
CPL US ARMY

ROY L BRYANT
PFC US ARMY

ROBERT C BUCHEIT
SFC US ARMY

FRANK BUNCHUK
SGT US ARMY

JOHN D BURGESS
SFC US ARMY

JOHN J BURKETT
MSG US ARMY

JOHN K BURROWS
1LT US ARMY

JAMES T BYRNE
SFC US ARMY

DOMINICK P
CALDARELLA
CPL US ARMY

JAMES C CALDWELL
SFC US ARMY

CARLIS J CALLAHAN
MSGT US ARMY

ARTHUR P CARLSEN
PVT US ARMY

PRIMO C CARNABUCI
CPL US ARMY

BENNY CARPENTER
CPL US ARMY

PATRICK T CASSATT
PFC US ARMY

WILLIAM E CAUTION
SFC US ARMY

JOHN S CAVAGNARO
CPL US ARMY

LEWIS W CHAMBERS
M/SGT US ARMY

MELVIN H CHANTRE
CPL US ARMY

RICHARD A CHAPPEL
CPL US ARMY

AUGUST D CITRONE
PFC US ARMY

GENE F CLARK
SGT US ARMY

WILLIAM L CLIFTON
PFC US ARMY

RICHARD D COKER
CPL US ARMY

CHARLES L COLEMAN
CPL US ARMY

WILLIAM K COLLINS
PFC US ARMY

SAMUEL W COMER
CWO US ARMY

ANTHONY E COSTA
SGT US ARMY

RAYMOND V COSTELLO
M/SGT US ARMY

HENRY G COSTELLO
CPL US ARMY

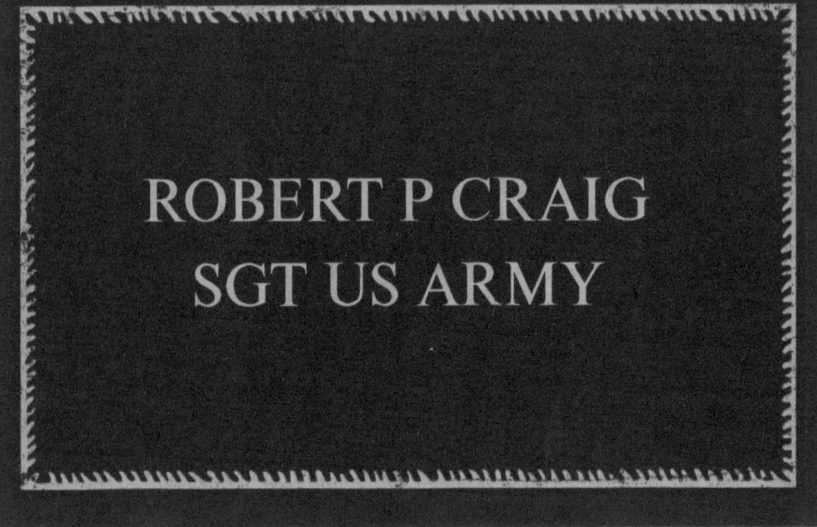

CLARENCE V COX
SFC US ARMY

ROBERT P CRAIG
SGT US ARMY

ASA J CRIMIN
SGT US ARMY

FLOYD T CRUMPTON
CPL US ARMY

ROBERT A G D'ALOISIO
SGT US ARMY

WILLIAM E DANTA
CPL US ARMY

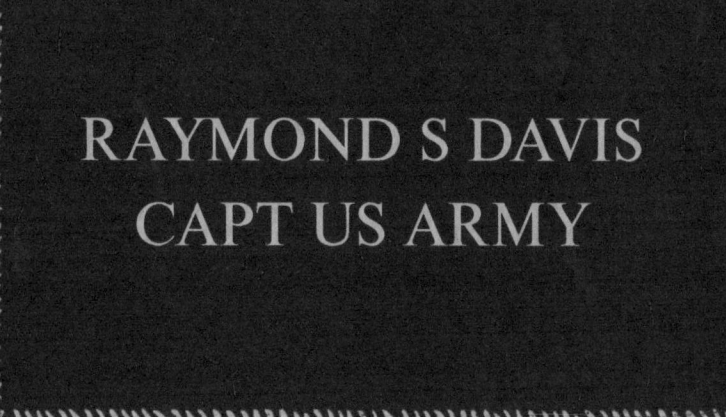

RICHARD DAVIS
M/SGT US ARMY

RAYMOND S DAVIS
CAPT US ARMY

ONLEY T DAVIS
CPT US ARMY

RICHARD F DAVIS
M/SGT US ARMY

SALVATORE DECOSTA
MSG US ARMY

RICHARD L DEMERS
PFC US ARMY

JAMES D DEWEY
SGT US ARMY

AGOSTINO DI RIENZO
SGT US ARMY

DANIEL J DI SYLVESTER
PFC US ARMY

EUGENE J DONNELLY
SGT US ARMY

N J DORCH
CPL US ARMY

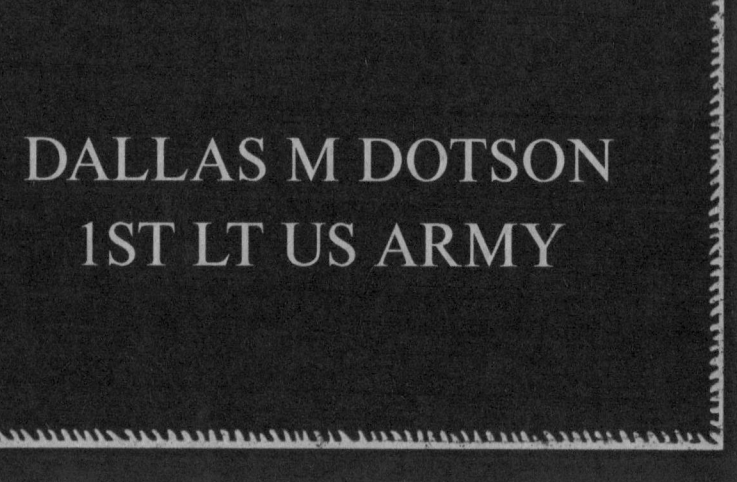

DALLAS M DOTSON
1ST LT US ARMY

ROBERT DULD
CPL US ARMY

JAMES R DUNN
SFC US ARMY

LOUIS J DUPLESSIS
CPL US ARMY

ELBYRNE O EARLY
SGT US ARMY

LEWIS W EBERNICKLE
PFC US ARMY

COLIN C ECCLES
CWO US ARMY

GERALD H EFFA
PFC US ARMY

DONALD C EFLAND
CPL US ARMY

WILLIAM C ENNIS
MSG US ARMY

ANDREW ERNANDIS
SGT US ARMY

DOUGALL H ESPEY
SGT US ARMY

BRYANT EVANS
CPL US ARMY

WILLIAM F FARRELL
SGT US ARMY

GRANT R FETROW
M/SGT US ARMY

CHARLES E FIDDLER
SGT US ARMY

WILLIAM H FISHER
CPL US ARMY

ROBERT J FOLEY
PFC US ARMY

RUSSELL J FOREMAN
CPL US ARMY

REGINALD E FRAZIER
PFC US ARMY

DONALD R FREEMAN
CPL US ARMY

WALTER H FREEMAN
CPL US ARMY

JACK L FRYE
CPL US ARMY

NORBERT W FRYMAN
CPL US ARMY

GERALD W FULLBRIGHT
SFC US ARMY

ROBERT R FUNKE
SFC US ARMY

NORMAN J FURMAN
CPL US ARMY

WALTER C FURTADO
SGT US ARMY

JAMES S GABLEHOUSE
PFC US ARMY

DALE R GARRISON
CPL US ARMY

DONALD B GEISLER
SGT US ARMY

PATRICK R GLENNON
CPL US ARMY

RALPH J GODBOUT
SGT US ARMY

RUBEN J GOMEZ
CPL US ARMY

ERVIN P GOTHIER
SGT US ARMY

WALTER W GREEN
PFC US ARMY

JOSEPH GREGORI
CPL US ARMY

ROBERT S GREGORY
SGT US ARMY

LEWIS A GUILDS
SFC US ARMY

VIRGIL GUY
SFC US ARMY

FLAVY C HAMRICK
CPL US ARMY

MEIDEL HANSEN
CPL US ARMY

HARRY E HARKNESS
SFC US ARMY

WAYNE E HARRIS
SFC US ARMY

MAJOR M HARRIS
CPL US ARMY

HARRY J HARTMANN
PFC US ARMY

GEORGE C HATTON
CPL US ARMY

WILLIAM M HEU
PFC US ARMY

CHARLES H HIGDON
PFC US ARMY

JAMES T HIGGINS
SGT US ARMY

EARL E HILGENBERG
SFC US ARMY

RICHARD H HOBART
CPL US ARMY

ROBERT W HOBSON
PFC US ARMY

JOHN L HOEY
PFC US ARMY

CLARENCE S HOGUE
SFC US ARMY

CHARLES E HOLTZCLAW
CPL US ARMY

ROBERT HOPKE
CPL US ARMY

HAMILTON P HORNER
CPL US ARMY

RAMON L HUBER
SFC US ARMY

RALPH M HUMMEL
PFC US ARMY

WARREN J INGLAND
CPL US ARMY

FRANCIS R JENKINS
M/SGT US ARMY

WALTER V JENSEN
SGT US ARMY

ELVIS J JIMES
PFC US ARMY

LEWIS H JOHNSON
CPL US ARMY

HARRY C JOHNSON
CPL US ARMY

WESLEY JOHNSON
PFC US ARMY

FRANK L JONES
SGT US ARMY

LOTCHIE J R JONES
PFC US ARMY

PAUL H JORDON
CAPT US ARMY

RICHARD A KANSKI
CPL US ARMY

EMIL J KAPAUN
CAPT US ARMY

RICHARD A KEAGLE
SFC US ARMY

WILLIAM R KEENAN
PFC US ARMY

JOHN C KELLER
SFC US ARMY

JOHN L KELLY
PFC US ARMY

LEONARD M KENNEDY
CPL US ARMY

ELVA L KEOPKE
MSG US ARMY

JAMES E KING
SFC US ARMY

MARTIN A KING
CPL US ARMY

MAXWELL D KITCHEN
CPL US ARMY

FRANK H KNOWLES
SGT US ARMY

JOHN KYLE
CPL US ARMY

DON M LA FOREST
SGT US ARMY

JOHN N LAPOINTE
CPL US ARMY

FRED A LAWSON
SGT US ARMY

ROLAND L LEBLANC
PFC US ARMY

RAY K LILLY
CPL US ARMY

FRANCIS E LINDSAY
SGT US ARMY

JOHN G LINKOWSKI
M/SGT US ARMY

CHARLES H LORD
PFC US ARMY

THEODORE E LOWERY
SFC US ARMY

ANDREW J LUCKETT
CPL US ARMY

BOB R MANKIN
SGT US ARMY

EARL H MARKLE
CPL US ARMY

JAMES F MARLAR
SFC US ARMY

JOHN MARONI
CPL US ARMY

CHARLES L MARR
CPL US ARMY

HARRY A MARSHALL
SFC US ARMY

CARL D MARTIN
M/SGT US ARMY

JOHN E MASKO
CPL US ARMY

HENRY D MATHUS
CPL US ARMY

JOSEPH J MATSUNAGA
SGT US ARMY

LINCOLN C MAY
SFC US ARMY

JOHN E MCCABE
PFC US ARMY

ALBERT A MCCARTHY
M/SGT US ARMY

RONALD J MCCOMB
PFC US ARMY

CHARLES H MCDANIEL
M/SGT US ARMY

ROBERT P MCDERMOND
CPL US ARMY

EDWARD N MCGAFFIC
CPL US ARMY

JAMES P MCGUIRE
SGT US ARMY

ROBERT H MCINTYRE
SGT US ARMY

HERBERT V MCKEEHAN
PFC US ARMY

JOHN L MCKENZIE
PFC US ARMY

DONALD L MCKEON
PFC US ARMY

JOSEPH L MCNALLY
MSG US ARMY

JOHN P MCQUADE
M/SGT US ARMY

ALFRED C MCWHIRTER
CPL US ARMY

ROGER F MEAGHER
1ST LT US ARMY

NEIL W MEAGHER
SGT US ARMY

CHARLES E MEYERS
PFC US ARMY

JOSEPH W MICK
CPL US ARMY

HOWARD A MILLER
1ST LT US ARMY

ROBERT F MILLER
CPL US ARMY

GERALD E MILLER
M/SGT US ARMY

BRUCE R MILLS
CPL US ARMY

ANGELO MONGIARDO
SFC US ARMY

ENOCH P MONTOYA
SGT US ARMY

BERNIE MONTOYA
SGT US ARMY

HAROLD B MOORE
CPL US ARMY

LEON M MOORE
CPL US ARMY

FRANK M MORALES
SGT US ARMY

ANDREW J MOREN
PFC US ARMY

FERNAND A MORIN
CPL US ARMY

ALBERT H MORRIS
PFC US ARMY

LESTER C MUELLER
MSG US ARMY

THOMAS H MULLINS
CPL US ARMY

DALE B NAGLE
CPL US ARMY

ARDELL N NEAL
CPL US ARMY

STEPHEN P NEMEC
CPL US ARMY

WILLIAM H NIXON
SGT US ARMY

LAWRENCE T NOLAN
SFC US ARMY

JOHN F NOWAK
SGT US ARMY

JAMES P O'LEARY
SGT US ARMY

WILLIAM T O'MALLEY
SGT US ARMY

RAYMOND G O'NEAL
CPL US ARMY

JOHN H OETJEN
CPL US ARMY

ALFRED D OGLESBY
CPL US ARMY

ROBERT J ORMOND
MAJ US ARMY

JOSEPH PAIVA
CPL US ARMY

JAMES R PALMER
CPL US ARMY

RAYMOND PARK
SGT US ARMY

ROBERT E PARNOW
SGT US ARMY

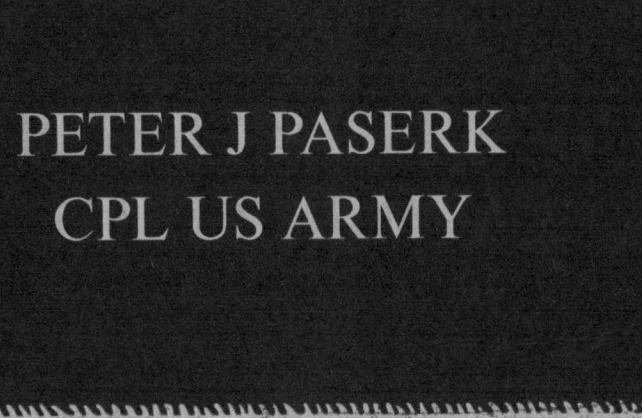

JOSE M PARRA
SFC US ARMY

PETER J PASERK
CPL US ARMY

ROBERT L PAULLEY
CPL US ARMY

LAWRENCE A PAULY
SGT US ARMY

GROVER C PEGG
M/SGT US ARMY

LELAND R PELLERIN
MAJ US ARMY

JULIO I PERRONE
CPL US ARMY

GEORGE W PETERBURS
CAPT US ARMY

WILLIAM F PETERS
CPL US ARMY

DAVID J PETHEL
SGT US ARMY

HARRY L PHELPS
CPL US ARMY

VIRGIL L PHILLIPS
SGT US ARMY

WALTER PIERCE
SGT US ARMY

EDWARD E PIERCE
PFC US ARMY

RUSSELL C PINNELL
SFC US ARMY

HAROLD L PINNELL
SFC US ARMY

EVERETT E POLLEN
CPL US ARMY

CECIL POORE
CPL US ARMY

FRED L POPPELL
SFC US ARMY

CLARENCE E
POSTLETHWAIT
CPL US ARMY

EDWARD J PRATT
SFC US ARMY

MERRITT L PRATT
M/SGT US ARMY

JAMES E PRICE
PFC US ARMY

ARMAND H PROULX
CPL US ARMY

JOSEPH S PURCELL
SGT US ARMY

JOHN F QUIGG
SGT US ARMY

DANIEL J RAVEN
PFC US ARMY

HARRY J REEVE
CPL US ARMY

ROBERT W REIGLE
CPL US ARMY

THEODORE A
REYNOLDS
CPL US ARMY

CLIFTON L RICE
SGT US ARMY

LESLIE K RICHARDSON
SGT US ARMY

JOHN E RIVERS
CPL US ARMY

MICHAEL ROBANKE
SFC US ARMY

GORDON A ROBERTS
M/SGT US ARMY

JOSEPH A ROBERTS
CPL US ARMY

RAYGER G ROBERTS
SGT US ARMY

JAMES B RODWAY
CPL US ARMY

BENNY D ROGERS
SFC US ARMY

VINCENZO D ROMEO
SGT US ARMY

NILS O RONNQUIST
SFC US ARMY

ARMAND G ROSSI
SGT US ARMY

WILLARD A RULE
SFC US ARMY

CLIFFORD L RYAN
M/SGT US ARMY

DARRELL W
SCARBROUGH
CPL US ARMY

GEORGE R SCHIPANI
SGT US ARMY

RALPH H SCHOOLEY
M/SGT US ARMY

DANIEL J SCHULTZ
CPL US ARMY

RICHARD J SCHULTZ
CPL US ARMY

DOMINIC N SCOCCHERA
SGT US ARMY

VERNON L SELVESTER
PFC US ARMY

VINCENT C SEMINARA
CPL US ARMY

GEORGE J SHANK
SFC US ARMY

RALPH L SHAW
SGT US ARMY

CHARLES H SHIPPEN
PFC US ARMY

JAMES P SHUNNEY
SFC US ARMY

GLEN L SHUPE
PFC US ARMY

LEWIS SIMPSON
SFC US ARMY

HOMER L SISK
CPL US ARMY

CHARLES E SIZEMORE
CPL US ARMY

JOSEPH J SKWIERAWSKI
SGT US ARMY

WALLACE SLIGHT
SFC US ARMY

DONALD L SMITH
CPL US ARMY

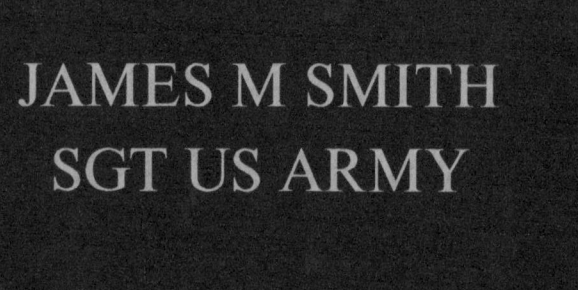

JAMES M SMITH
SGT US ARMY

CLARENCE D SMITH
M/SGT US ARMY

JOHN S SMITH
PVT US ARMY

VERNON D SMITH
SGT US ARMY

PAUL T SMITH
PFC US ARMY

SHADRACH B SMITH
SGT US ARMY

HARRY S SMITH
SFC US ARMY

FRANK S SMOLINSKY
CPL US ARMY

CLARENCE O
SMOTHERMON
SFC US ARMY

RONALD SNOW
CPL US ARMY

DAVID L SNYDER
CPL US ARMY

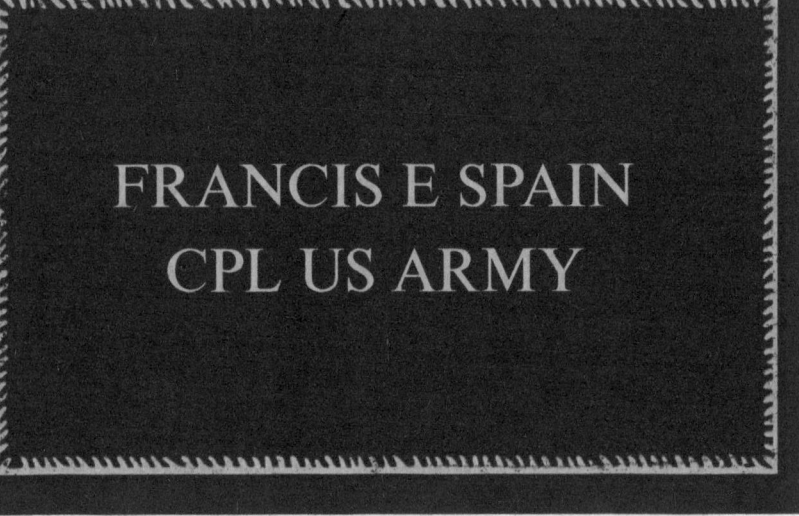

ERNEST T SOCHA
CPL US ARMY

FRANCIS E SPAIN
CPL US ARMY

GEORGE L
SPANGENBERG
PFC US ARMY

DONALD E SPANGLER
PFC US ARMY

HAROLD SPARKS
SGT US ARMY

RUSSELL L SPEGAL
SGT US ARMY

JOHN C SPELLMAN
CPL US ARMY

ELMO M SPILLER
PFC US ARMY

ROBERT W SPRINGBORN
CPL US ARMY

KENNETH R STADLER
SGT US ARMY

FRANCIS H STAMER
M/SGT US ARMY

HAROLD C STAMM
SGT US ARMY

THEODORE STANKS
PFC US ARMY

WILLIAM T STEWART
CPL US ARMY

ROBERT J STIM
SGT US ARMY

ROBERT B STRAIGHT
MAJ US ARMY

MARVIN B STRICKLAND
CPL US ARMY

JOHN O STROM
CPL US ARMY

WILLIAM A STRONG
PFC US ARMY

EDWARD C STRYLOWSKI
M/SGT US ARMY

KENNETH R STUCK
CPL US ARMY

PETER P SUKLEY
CPL US ARMY

JAMES E SULSER
PFC US ARMY

CONRAD E SUTPHIN
PFC US ARMY

LESLIE R SUTTON
CPL US ARMY

DEAN E TAYLOR
CPL US ARMY

JOSEPH A TERRELL
PFC US ARMY

CHARLES C THOMAS
SFC US ARMY

ODGEN N THOMPSON
SFC US ARMY

CHESTER T
THRAILKILL
SGT US ARMY

ANTONIO D TIJERINA
CPL US ARMY

DONALD E TIPPERY
CPL US ARMY

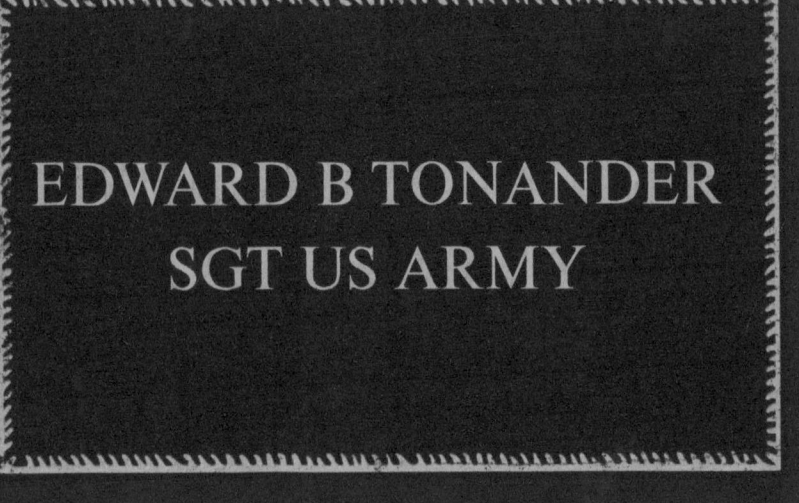

LEO C TODD
SGT US ARMY

EDWARD B TONANDER
SGT US ARMY

ELIAS E TORRES
CPL US ARMY

IRVING
TOURTELLOTTE
SGT US ARMY

JESSE J TRAUGHBER
CPL US ARMY

CLARENCE W TRIVETT
CPL US ARMY

JAMES K TUTTLE
CPL US ARMY

TROY D UNDERWOOD
SGT US ARMY

JOSEPH P
URBANORWICZ
CPL US ARMY

JOE D URIBE
PFC US ARMY

CIRILDO VALENCIO
M/SGT US ARMY

BOB S VALERA
M/SGT US ARMY

EDWARD L R
VAN DUSEN
CPL US ARMY

MANUEL N VELA
PFC US ARMY

ROBERT A WAGNER
1ST LT US ARMY

REX E WAGNER
CPL US ARMY

MAX E WALLS
CPL US ARMY

JAMES J WALSH
SFC US ARMY

GEORGE W WALTERS
CPL US ARMY

ELMER E WALTZ
CPL US ARMY

ALFRED E WARMOUTH
PFC US ARMY

T P WARREN
SFC US ARMY

RICHARD C WASINGER
CPL US ARMY

CARL W WATERBURY
M/SGT US ARMY

JAMES E WATTS
SGT US ARMY

ROGER J WEAVER
SGT US ARMY

RAYMOND D WENDELL
CPL US ARMY

CHESTER WENTKO
CPL US ARMY

JOHN W WEST
SGT US ARMY

FREDERICK W WHALEN
CPL US ARMY

JOHN H WHEELER
CPL US ARMY

JOHN H WHITE
SGT US ARMY

CHARLES P WHITLER
SGT US ARMY

MAURICE E WILHELM
CAPT US ARMY

CECIL M WILLIS
SGT US ARMY

LINWOOD F D WILSON
PFC US ARMY

JAMES R WILSON
CPL US ARMY

SILAS W WILSON
M/SGT US ARMY

CHARLES E WILSON
CPL US ARMY

JAMES D WISE
CPL US ARMY

LUTHER WISE
M/SGT US ARMY

WILLIAM E WOOD
CPL US ARMY

EDWIN E WOOTEN
CPL US ARMY

LEO B YELLE
SFC US ARMY

RICHARD A YERNAUX
SGT US ARMY

MANUEL G ZARAGOZA
SFC US ARMY

MARVIN H ZEMPEL
PFC US ARMY

They were sons.
Brothers.
Uncles.

We remember them—
for the battles they fought,
and the futures they never lived.

Leland. John. James. Benjamin. Albert.
Joseph.
And more than a thousand others.

At Unsan, they stood.

May we live lives worthy of their sacrifice.
Earn this.